ALMA FLOR ADA ✻ F. ISABEL CAMPOY

Scenes from

ROLL 'N' ROLE

 Illustrators

MARÍA EUGENIA JARA

Jenny Hen

CLAUDIA LEGNAZZI

Serafina's Birthday

FELIPE UGALDE

The Friendly Ant

ALFAGUARA

YOUNG READERS

Originally published in Spanish as *Teatrín de Don Crispín*

Text ©2001 Alma Flor Ada and F. Isabel Campoy
Edition ©2001 Santillana USA Publishing Company, Inc.

Santillana USA Publishing Company, Inc.
2105 NW 86th Avenue
Miami, FL 33122

Alfaguara is part of the **Santillana Group**,
with offices in the following countries:

ARGENTINA, BOLIVIA, CHILE, COLOMBIA, COSTA RICA,
DOMINICAN REPUBLIC, ECUADOR, EL SALVADOR,
GUATEMALA, MEXICO, PANAMA, PERU, PUERTO RICO,
SPAIN, UNITED STATES, URUGUAY AND VENEZUELA.

ISBN: 1-58105-678-8

Theater B: *Roll 'n' Role*

Translator: Sandra Arnold
Editorial: Norman Duarte, Adam Sugerman,
 W. Leland Northam, Isabel Mendoza,
 Claudia Baca
Art Director: Felipe Dávalos
Design: Petra Ediciones

ILLUSTRATORS
MARÍA EUGENIA JARA: pp. 6–13
CLAUDIA LEGNAZZI: pp. 14–25
FELIPE UGALDE: pp. 5, 26–32

CONTENTS

For Diego, Conchi-Loli, and José;
for Oscar and Arturo Coronado
—each a lover and beloved of the theater.

Raise the Curtain!

Somewhere in your house,
can you find a coat,
a tie,
or a briefcase,
that can turn you into a teacher?

Can you find a piece of cloth that
can be used as a curtain?
Can you find a hat
or maybe a walking stick?

If you can find these things,
dig down inside yourself
for the words to say,
and let the performance
begin!

Jenny Hen
New version by F. Isabel Campoy

CHARACTERS
NARRATOR
MR. ROOSTER
THREE PIGLETS
JENNY HEN
CHICKS
MR. WOLF

Narrator:
There once was a farm where all lived happily.

Mr. Rooster:
Cock-a-doodle-doo. Good morning, dear friends!

First Piglet:
Oink.

Second Piglet:
Oink, oink.

Third Piglet:
Oink, oink, oink.

Narrator:

But the happiest of all was
Jenny Hen. She liked to sew.

Jenny Hen:

Has anyone seen my white apron?
Has anyone seen my scissors and my white thread?

Narrator:

Jenny had an apron. In her apron, she
had a small pocket. In the pocket, she
had a thimble, a pair of scissors, and
many different colors of thread for her embroidery.

Chicks:

Your apron is hanging by the door.

Piglets:

It is hanging by the door.

Mr. Rooster:

By the door! By the door!

Narrator:

Jenny sewed and sang.
While she sewed and sang,
she didn't notice anything around her.
She sewed and sewed
and didn't realize
Mr. Wolf was watching her.

Mr. Wolf:

What a beautiful little hen!
I'll take her home and eat her for dinner.

Narrator:

And with a swipe, horrible Mr. Wolf
put Jenny in his sack and carried her away.

Mr. Wolf:

What a beautiful hen!
I'll take her to my den.
I'll put her in a pot
and turn the stove on hot.

Narrator:

So the wolf trudged along mile after mile.
When he got to the forest, he said:

Mr. Wolf:

This is such a heavy sack! I am going to take a rest.

Narrator:

Mr. Wolf fell asleep and began to snore.

Mr. Wolf: *(snoring)*
Agh zzz! Agh zzz!

Narrator:
Jenny Hen was terrified inside the sack.
She remembered her apron, her scissors,
her thimble, and her embroidery thread.

Jenny Hen: *(softly)*
I'll cut the sack open,
and I'll put a rock inside.
I'll sew the sack up,
and I'll run away as fast as I can.

Narrator:
And that is what she did.
When Mr. Wolf woke up,
he heaved the sack
onto his shoulder
and went on his way.

Narrator:

When Mr. Wolf got home, he put a pot
filled with water on the stove to heat.
While chopping some onions, he sang:

Mr. Wolf:

What a beautiful hen!
She's here in my den.
I'll put her in a pot
and turn the stove on hot.

Narrator:

When the water was very hot, so hot
that it bubbled over, Mr. Wolf lifted
the sack to dump the hen in the pot.
Plop! The rock splashed him
with boiling water.

Mr. Wolf:

Help! Help!

Narrator:

Mr. Wolf ran out screaming and whimpering:

Mr. Wolf:

Burned by my stew!
What can I do?
Scalded by my hen with onion,
from my head to my bunion.

Serafina's Birthday

by Alma Flor Ada

CHARACTERS
SEBASTIAN RABBIT
SERAFINA RABBIT
TRAIN CONDUCTOR
A CAT
A DOG
THREE SQUIRRELS
WHITE RABBIT
CINNAMON RABBIT
CHESTNUT RABBIT

ACT 1

In Sebastian's house.

*(The alarm clock rings.
Sebastian gets up in a hurry.
He looks at the clock and
runs around.)*

Sebastian:

It's late, very late.
How is this possible?
If I don't hurry,
I'll miss the train.

14

Sebastian: *(He is about to leave the house when he returns to brush his teeth.)* It's unheard-of for a rabbit to leave the house without brushing his teeth.

(The train whistle is heard.)

Sebastian: *(running)* I can't miss that train.

ACT 2

On the train.

Sebastian: *(upset)*
I can't believe it!
I left Serafina's present at home.
It's unheard-of for a rabbit to go
to his best friend's birthday party
without a present.

Sebastian: *(taking his coin pouch out)*
At least, I didn't forget my coin pouch.
I'll buy her a present.

Conductor:
Five minutes to Rabbit Village.

ACT 3

In Rabbit Village.

Sebastian: *(sad, head down)*
All the stores are closed.
What am I going to do?
It's unheard-of for a rabbit to go
to his best friend's birthday party
without a present.

(*Sebastian comes upon a lettuce garden.*)

Sebastian:
Lettuce!
Great!
Serafina loves lettuce.

Dog: (*barking ferociously*)
If you value your hide,
don't even think about coming in here!

(*Scared, Sebastian runs away fast.*)

Sebastian:
What a shame!
I thought I had found a present.

(Sebastian comes upon a cabbage patch.)

Sebastian:
Serafina doesn't like cabbage a lot.
But since there is no lettuce, cabbage
will do.

*(When he approaches the cabbages,
a scary cat appears.)*

Cat: *(hissing angrily)*
If you value your life,
don't even think of coming in here!

(Sebastian is frightened and leaves quickly.)

ACT 4

In the forest.

Sebastian: *(catching his breath under a tree)*
I am glad I ran away from that dog and cat.
But what a shame! I won't be able to take
Serafina even a head of cabbage.
It's unheard-of for a rabbit not to have a
present for his best friend.

(A walnut hits him on the head. Sebastian realizes that he is under a walnut tree filled with walnuts. Many walnuts cover the ground.)

Sebastian:

It's a good thing I have found something! I will take her some walnuts.

(He begins to fill his cap with nuts. Several angry squirrels appear.)

First Squirrel:

Thief! Don't steal our walnuts!

Second Squirrel:

They are ours! All ours!

Third Squirrel:

We save them for winter. They are our children's food.

(Sebastian empties his cap and he walks away with his head down.)

ACT 5

At Serafina's house.

(There are birthday decorations and several dressed up rabbits. Serafina paces back and forth and looks out the window.)

Serafina:

I can't believe Sebastian is not coming to my party.

White Rabbit:

He is very forgetful. He forgets everything!

Serafina:

I know he forgets everything, but I am his best friend! He couldn't have forgotten my birthday.

Cinnamon Rabbit:

The worst of all is that Grandpa couldn't come to tell us stories.

Serafina:

A party without Sebastian and without Grandpa's stories is not a party.

(There is a knock at the door and Serafina runs to open it. It's Sebastian all a mess, sweaty, dusty, and sad.)

Serafina:

Sebastian! You finally arrived!
I knew you wouldn't forget.
But what is the matter?

Sebastian:

You can't imagine everything
that has happened to me...
I am very embarrassed.
I haven't brought a present.
It's unheard-of for a rabbit
to come to a birthday party
without a present.

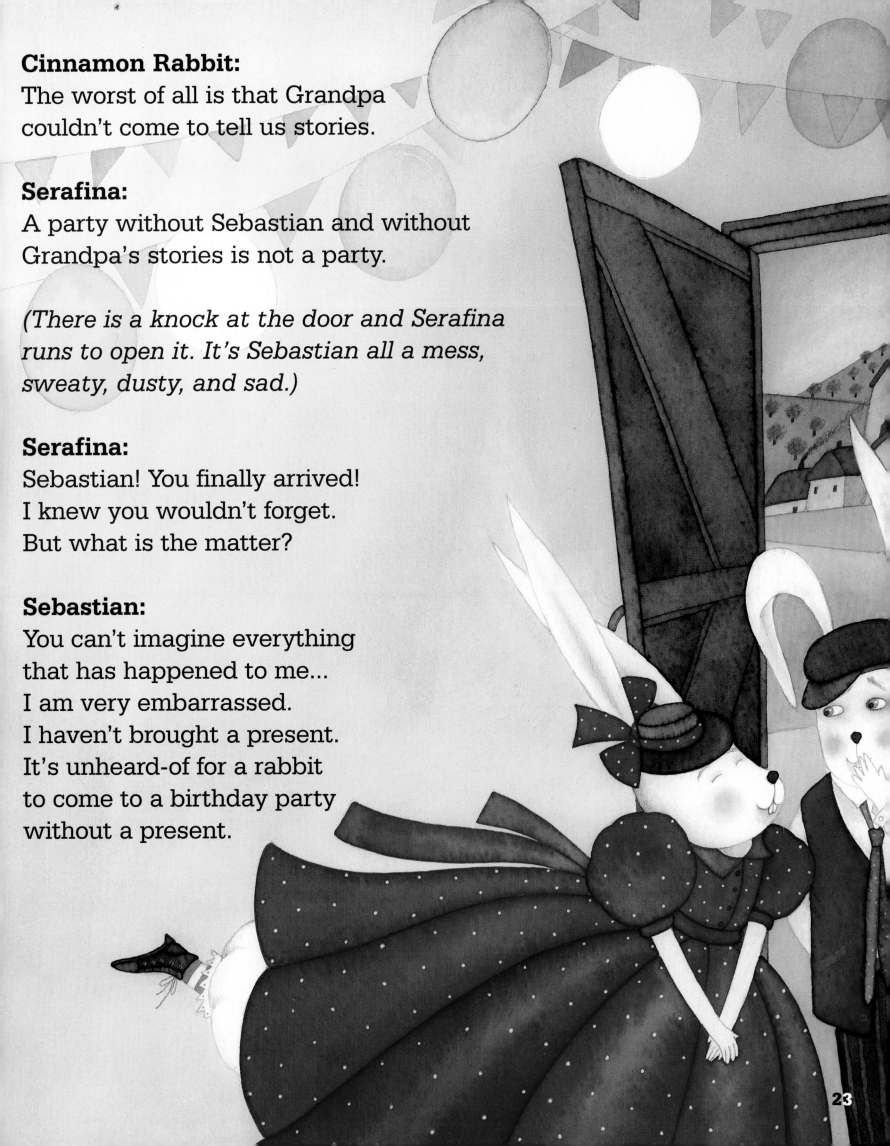

Chestnut Rabbit:
Come, sit here in Grandpa's chair.
Tell us everything that has happened to you.

Sebastian:
Well, everything began this morning when the alarm went off. I realized that I hadn't set it right, and I wouldn't be able to catch the train on time...

*(Sebastian continues talking, moving his hands,
although the audience can't hear.)*

Serafina: *(enthusiastically)*
And you said you didn't have a present.
You brought us the best present
of all: a story!

The Friendly Ant

Theatrical version by F. Isabel Campoy and Alma Flor Ada

CHARACTERS
NARRATOR
KATYDID
SPARROW
WOODPECKER
MS. ANT
OLD SQUIRREL
QUEEN BEE

Narrator:

After a long cold winter
and a rainy spring,
summer came at last.

Katydid:

How I love it!
After the spring,
all through the summer,
I sing, sing, sing.

Ribet, sang the frog.
Ribet, deep in the bog.
Ribet, a gentleman went by.
Ribet, with a hat and a tie.

Sparrow:

Katydid, you sing so joyfully!

Woodpecker:

The whole pine grove is happy!

Ms. Ant:

Yes, yes, but in the winter,
what will you eat?

Katydid:

I have a doll
all dressed in blue,
with a silken scarf
and shiny white shoes.
I took her for a walk,
and a bad cold she caught.
So I put her to bed,
and stroked her fevered head.
This morning the doctor
told me what to do:
a forkful of syrup
and she'll feel brand new.

Narrator:

And that is the way
it was every morning:
the ants working
and the katydid
singing.

Ms. Ant:

Oh! I'm so tired.
Every day, up and down,
up and down,
looking for food for winter.

Katydid:

Ms. Ant, my good friend.
Sing with me this new song.
I come to sing to my friend, the sun.

The day you were born,
beautiful things
appeared in the blue.
The sun, the moon,
and the stars were born, too.

Ms. Ant:
I would like to sit up
in that tree and sing,
but I have work to do.

Narrator:
The days would come and go,
the ants working
and the katydid singing.

Narrator:
Fall came,
and then came winter.
Snow fell. All the animals were
inside their houses.

Old Squirrel:
Come to the table,
my little squirrels.
We have pine nuts for
dinner tonight.

Queen Bee:
Come to the table, my little bees.
We have pollen and honey for
dinner tonight.

Narrator:
All the animals had something
to eat, except—the katydid.

Katydid: *(shivering)*
Brrrr, it's so cold!
I have nothing to eat.
What am I going to do?

Narrator:
Feeling very ashamed,
the katydid knocked
on Ms. Ant's door.

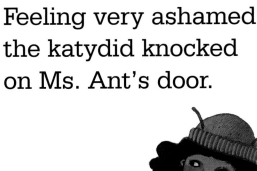

Katydid:
Ms. Ant, could you give me
something to eat?
The fields are covered
with snow, and there is nothing
to be found. I know you warned me...

Ms. Ant:
The truth is, Katydid, my friend,
I have missed your singing
in the darkness of my anthill.
Now I realize how happy
it made me to listen to you.
Come in, come in.

Narrator:
And that is how it came to pass
that the ant gave shelter to
the katydid in her cozy anthill.
She invited the katydid to eat the food,
and the katydid sang
to brighten the long winter days.
Her singing brought back
the fragrance of the flowers,
and filled the anthill
with bright sunshine.